This edition published by Parragon Books Ltd in 2016

Parragon
Chartist House
15–17 Trim Street
Bath BA1 1HA, UK
www.parragon.com

ISBN 978-1-4723-2523-5

Printed in China

From the movie

DISNEY

FROZEN

PaRragon

Bath • New York • Cologne • Melbourne • Delhi
Hong Kong • Shenzhen • Singapore

The kingdom of Arendelle was a busy and happy place, nestled among the mountains of the far north. At night, the colourful northern lights often lit up the sky in beautiful patterns.

A kind king and queen ruled Arendelle. Their young daughters, Elsa and Anna, were the joy of their lives. But the royal couple had a secret worry....

Their eldest daughter,
Elsa, had a magical power.
She could create snow and
freeze things with her hands!

Anna, the younger daughter, adored her big sister.
The two were inseparable. One night, Anna convinced
Elsa to sneak into the Great Hall in the castle and
create a winter wonderland!

But while the girls were playing, Elsa accidentally hit Anna with a blast of icy magic. Little Anna fell to the ground, shivering. A streak of white appeared in her hair. Frightened for her sister, Elsa called out for help.

The worried king and queen rushed their daughters to the realm of trolls. The trolls were mysterious healers who knew about magic.

A wise old troll spoke to them. "You are lucky it wasn't her heart that was struck," he said. "The heart is not so easily changed, but the head can be persuaded. We should remove all magic, even memories of magic, to be safe."

The old troll was able to cure Anna by changing her memories, removing all magic from her mind. This meant she wouldn't remember Elsa's magical power.

The troll warned the king and queen: "Fear will be your enemy."

Back in Arendelle, the king and queen felt more worried than ever. They locked the castle gates and taught Elsa to control her powers so that no one would find out about them. But whenever she had strong feelings, the magic spilled out. So the king gave her a pair of gloves to help hold it back.

Elsa decided that to keep Anna safe, it would be best to stay away from her.

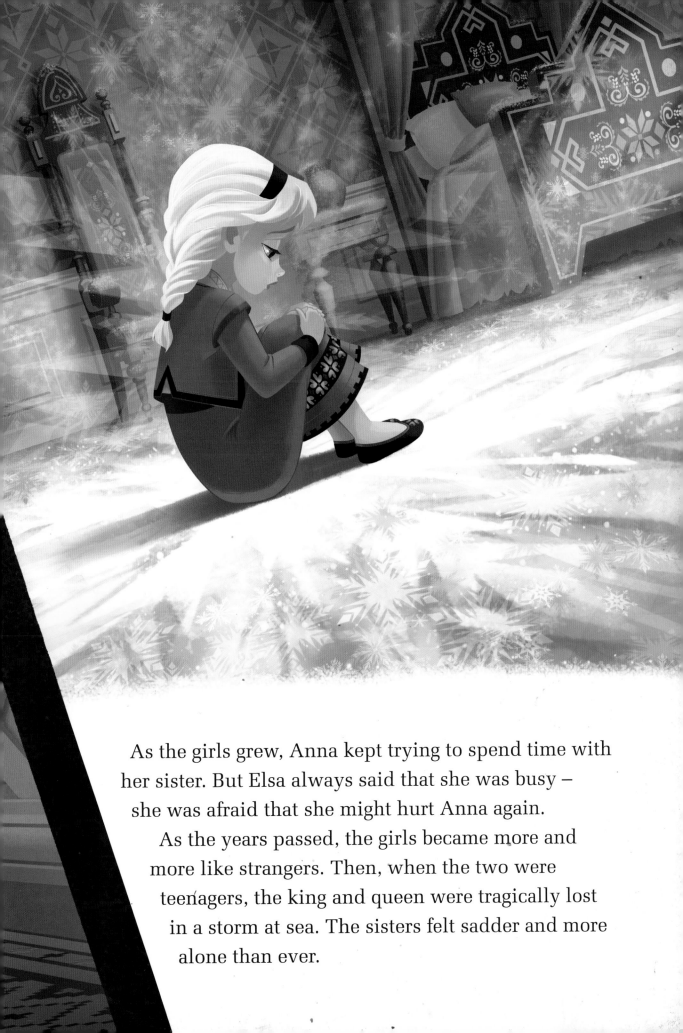

As the girls grew, Anna kept trying to spend time with
her sister. But Elsa always said that she was busy –
she was afraid that she might hurt Anna again.
As the years passed, the girls became more and
more like strangers. Then, when the two were
teenagers, the king and queen were tragically lost
in a storm at sea. The sisters felt sadder and more
alone than ever.

When Elsa was old enough, it was her turn to become queen. The gates to the castle were opened for one day only, to celebrate her coronation.

Anna was excited to meet so many people – especially a handsome young prince named Hans!

But Elsa was still struggling to hide her powers.
She just hoped that she could make it through the
day without anybody finding out about them.

To Elsa's relief, the celebration went exactly as planned. Everybody cheered for their beautiful new queen.

Afterwards, a party was held in the Great Hall. Anna and Prince Hans spent the evening laughing, dancing and talking. They had so much in common! Everything seemed perfect, so they made a big decision....

Anna introduced Hans to Elsa – and announced that they were going to be married.

Elsa was shocked. "You can't marry a man you just met," she told Anna.

"You can if it's true love," Anna insisted.

But Elsa would not listen to Anna's arguments. "My answer is no," she said firmly. "The party is over!"

Elsa started to leave the room, but Anna grabbed her hand – she was trying to make Elsa stay and talk. But Anna accidentally pulled off her sister's glove!

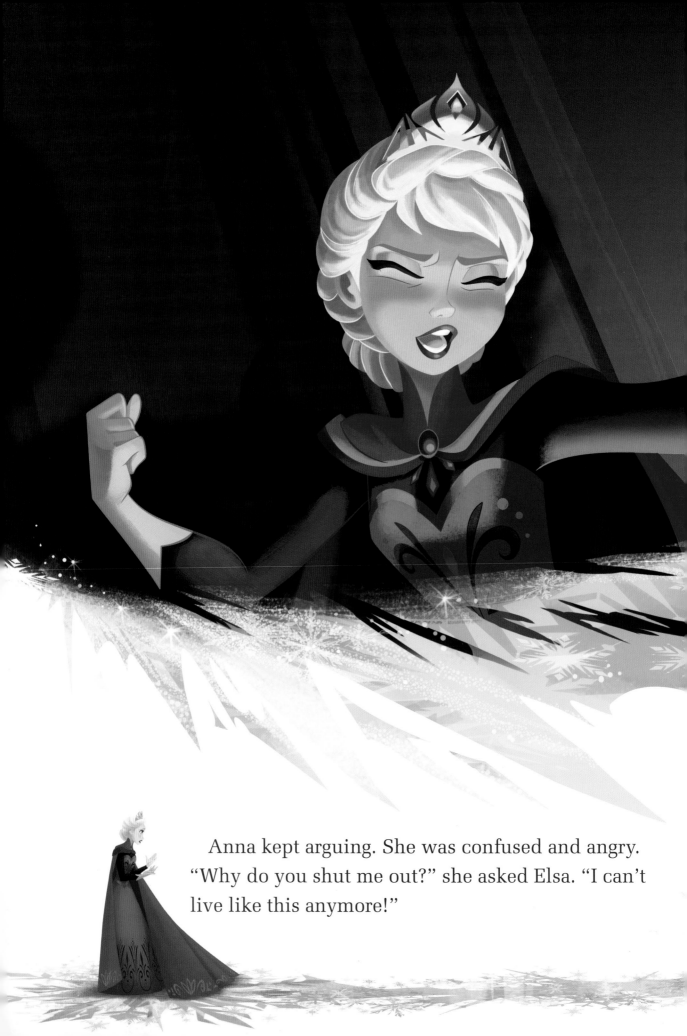

Anna kept arguing. She was confused and angry. "Why do you shut me out?" she asked Elsa. "I can't live like this anymore!"

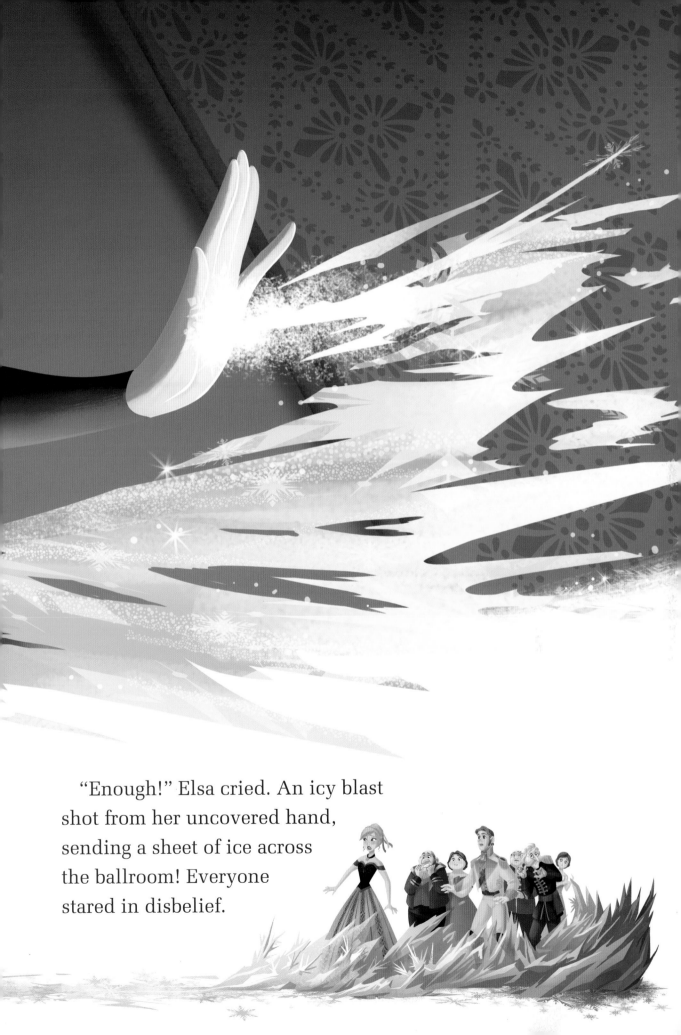

"Enough!" Elsa cried. An icy blast
shot from her uncovered hand,
sending a sheet of ice across
the ballroom! Everyone
stared in disbelief.

Elsa fled the castle, devastated that her secret had
finally been revealed and terrified that she might
hurt someone.

"Stay away from me!" she warned the townspeople.

Everything around Elsa turned to ice as she ran.
She stepped onto the fjord and the water froze solid!
She raced towards the mountains on the other side.

Elsa climbed into the mountains, and with nobody around to worry about, she let all of her power loose for the first time. She felt free! A blizzard flew around her. She even transformed her own dress into a beautiful icy gown.

As she neared the top of the mountain Elsa created a magnificent, shining ice palace. At last, she felt like the person she was always meant to be!

The building was *Wandering Oaken's Trading Post and Sauna*. Anna rushed in and immediately gathered up some supplies.

A young man named Kristoff was also collecting winter supplies. He mentioned that the storm was coming from the North Mountain.

Anna began asking questions. If the storm was on the North Mountain, Elsa would be there, too!

But Kristoff was busy bargaining for supplies. Feeling crowded, he finally blurted out, "Now back up, while I deal with this crook!" The insulted shopkeeper threw him out empty-handed into the snow.

This gave Anna an idea. She found Kristoff in the stable with his reindeer, Sven, and offered to give him the supplies he needed. In return, she asked that he take her up the North Mountain.

Finally, Kristoff agreed. "We leave at dawn."

"No," said Anna. "We leave right *now*."

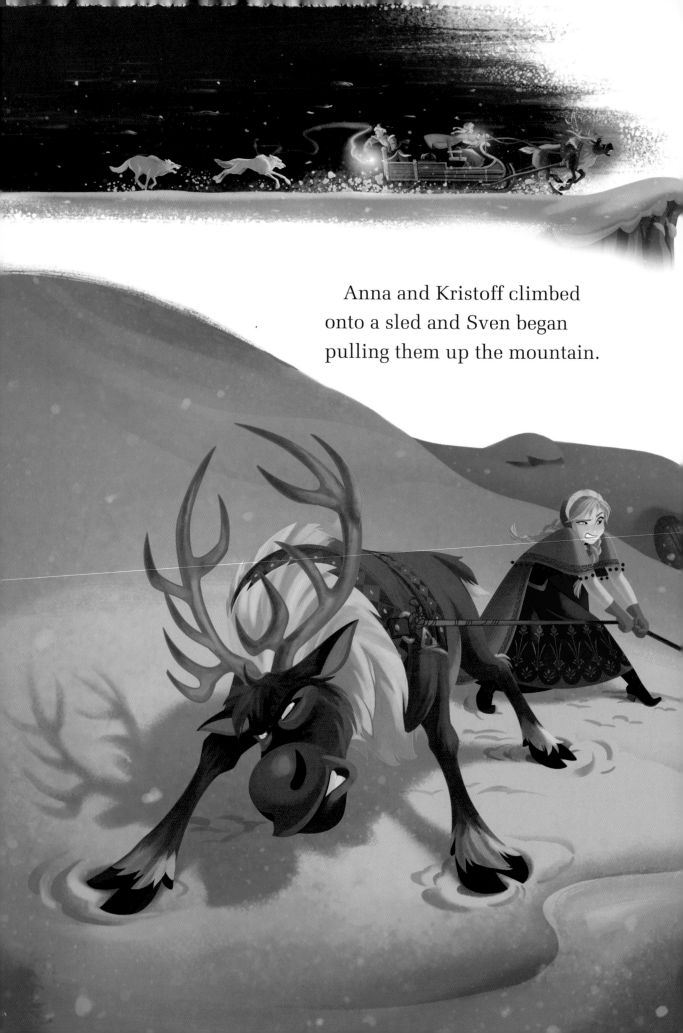

Anna and Kristoff climbed
onto a sled and Sven began
pulling them up the mountain.

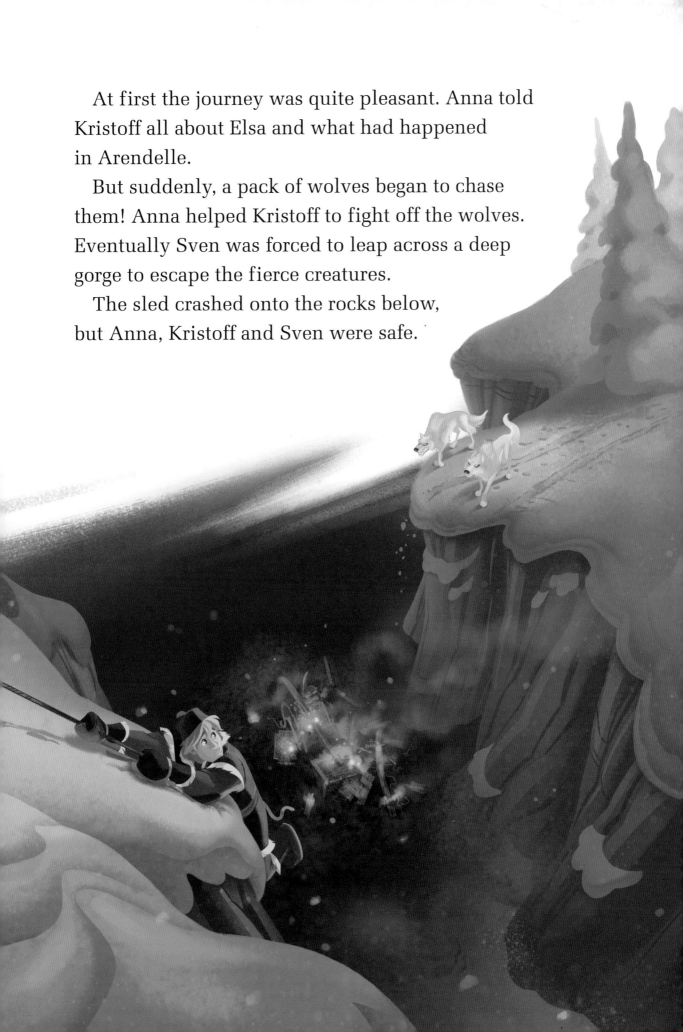

At first the journey was quite pleasant. Anna told Kristoff all about Elsa and what had happened in Arendelle.

But suddenly, a pack of wolves began to chase them! Anna helped Kristoff to fight off the wolves. Eventually Sven was forced to leap across a deep gorge to escape the fierce creatures.

The sled crashed onto the rocks below, but Anna, Kristoff and Sven were safe.

The trio continued into the forest on foot. They soon
came across a beautiful winter scene. Anna was more
eager than ever to find Elsa – she had to know more
about her sister's amazing power!

"I never knew winter could be so ... beautiful,"
Anna said.

"But it's so white," added a voice. "How about some colour?"

It was a living snowman!

"I'm Olaf," he said, explaining that Elsa had made him.

Anna gave Olaf a carrot nose, then asked him to lead them to her sister. "We need Elsa to bring back summer."

Olaf grinned. "I've always loved the idea of summer," he said. "The warm sun on my face, getting a gorgeous tan. Just doing whatever snow does in summer."

But Anna and Kristoff were both thinking the same thing: summer would *not* be a good thing for a snowman.

Elsa was worried to see Anna. She wanted to return home with her sister, but she knew that everything would be different now that her secret was out. She also remembered how dangerous her powers could be.

"I think you should go, Anna," Elsa said. "I'm sorry. It has to be this way."

But Anna explained that Arendelle was still frozen. If Elsa stayed away, everyone in the kingdom would freeze to death!

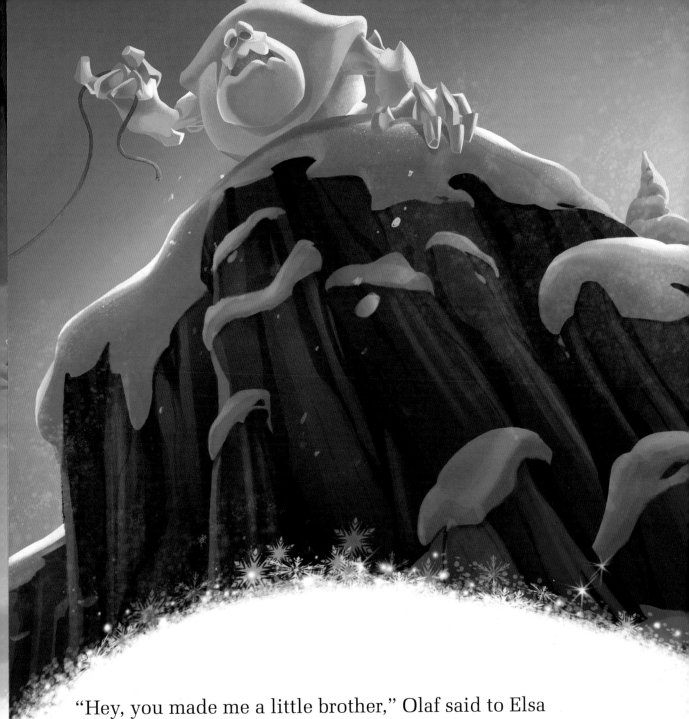

"Hey, you made me a little brother," Olaf said to Elsa happily. He turned to the huge snowman. "I'm going to name you Marshmallow!"

Elsa ordered Marshmallow to escort Anna and her companions off the mountain. But after Anna hit him with a snowball, he decided to chase them, instead!

The friends ran until they reached a cliff and then lowered themselves down the side. But Marshmallow grabbed the rope and pulled them back up. Anna did the only thing she could think of – she cut the rope!

Night fell as Kristoff led Anna and Olaf to the realm of the trolls. Seeing Kristoff, the trolls came out of hiding. Kristoff had spent a lot of time with them as he grew up, so he was practically family!

When an old troll touched Anna's hair, he understood immediately that she had been hurt. "There is ice in your heart, put there by your sister," the old troll said. He explained that Anna would freeze to solid ice forever in one day's time unless the magic was reversed. "Only an act of true love can thaw a frozen heart."

Thinking quickly, Olaf and Kristoff decided to take Anna back home. Surely, Prince Hans could break the spell with a true love's kiss.

Back in Arendelle, Hans had become worried when Anna's horse had returned without her. So he had gathered volunteers to help him find Anna.

When Hans's group arrived at the ice palace, Elsa tried to protect herself. But in the struggle, she was hit by falling ice and knocked out. She ended up being taken back to Arendelle as a prisoner.

But Hans made no move to kiss her. "Could it be this easy?" he asked, his smile turning into a sneer.

Then Hans put out the fire with a jug of water. He explained that he had only been pretending to be in love with her so that he could rule Arendelle!

With Anna nearly frozen, Hans saw that his dream was within reach. All he had to do now was get rid of Elsa.

"You can't," Anna gasped. She collapsed to the floor as the ice slowly spread through her body.

Meanwhile, imprisoned in the castle dungeon, all Elsa could think about was getting away from the kingdom, to protect everyone from her powers. She was also worried about Anna – she didn't know that Anna was back in Arendelle, too.

Elsa became so upset that she lost control of her magic and froze the dungeon. The ice broke her chains and she escaped!

With all of her remaining strength, Anna threw herself in front of Elsa. Hans's sword came down just as Anna's body froze to solid ice. With a loud CLANK, the blade shattered.

Elsa wept as she wrapped her arms around her sister. "Oh, Anna," she sobbed.

A moment passed. Then something amazing happened. Anna began to thaw! "Elsa?" she whispered.

"You sacrificed yourself for me?" Elsa asked. Anna nodded weakly.

"An act of true love will thaw a frozen heart," Olaf said.

With her sacrifice, Anna had helped Elsa to see that love was more powerful than fear.

Suddenly, Elsa realized that love was the force that could control her powers. She raised her arms and the ice and snow that covered Arendelle melted away.

But Olaf was melting, too! Elsa quickly made a little snow cloud just for him.

"This is the best day of my life!" he said.

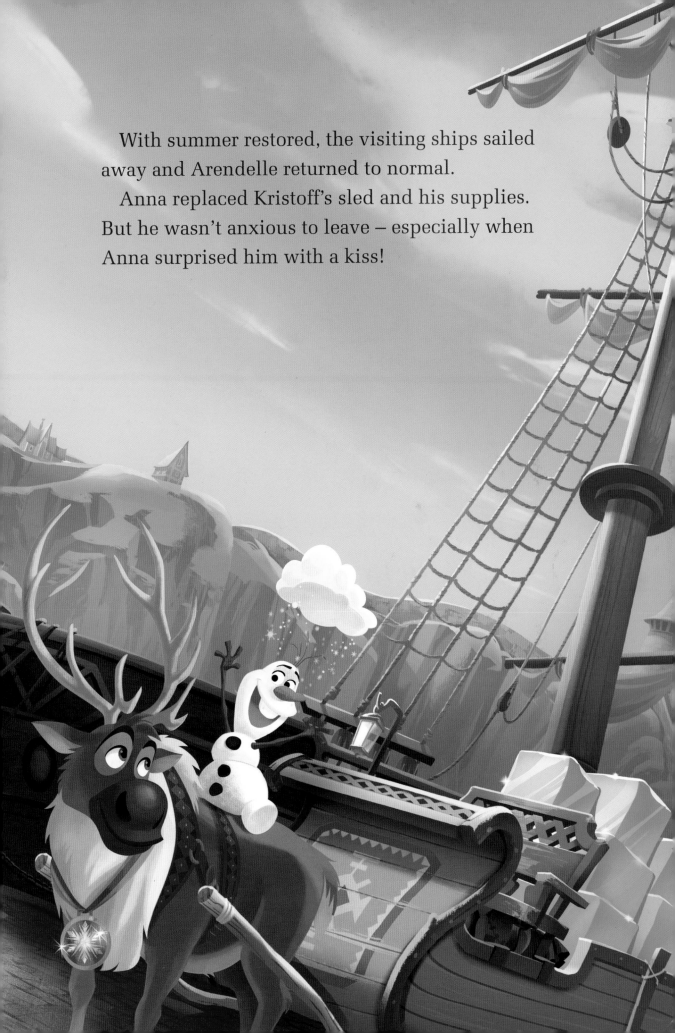

With summer restored, the visiting ships sailed
away and Arendelle returned to normal.

Anna replaced Kristoff's sled and his supplies.
But he wasn't anxious to leave – especially when
Anna surprised him with a kiss!

Elsa created an
ice-skating rink in the castle
and threw open the gates of the
kingdom – she never planned to close
them again.

Everyone had a wonderful time skating with
Queen Elsa and Princess Anna. The kingdom of
Arendelle was a happy place once more!

Anna and Elsa knew that
they would never let anything
come between them again.